Can we use it again?

T0364585

Written by Katie Foufouti
Illustrated by Roy Hermelin

Collins

What's in this book?

Listen and say

plastic bottle

can

paper

Download the audio at www.collins.co.uk/839713

box

5

Look! Lots of food cans.

What can we make?

You can put your pens and pencils in a can.

Draw a picture on some paper. Put it on a can. These candles are in cans.

candle

Look at these plastic bottles.

What can we make?

Look! A plastic bottle cow.
You can put coins in this cow.

coin

You can put pegs in a plastic bottle.

pegs

These flowers are in plastic bottles!
You can put them on a wall.

You can put food for birds in
a plastic bottle.

Look! Lots of big boxes!

What can we make?

These boxes are houses for dolls.
I like the doors and windows.

Cats and dogs love boxes.
They are good beds for them!

There are lots of things you can make.

Picture dictionary

Listen and repeat

can

candle

coin

peg

plastic bottle

1 Look and match

plastic bottle

box

can

2 Listen and say

Collins

Published by Collins
An imprint of HarperCollins*Publishers*
Westerhill Road
Bishopbriggs
Glasgow
G64 2QT

HarperCollins*Publishers*
Macken House, 39/40 Mayor Street Upper,
Dublin 1
DO1 C9W8
Ireland

William Collins' dream of knowledge for all began with the publication of his first book in 1819.

A self-educated mill worker, he not only enriched millions of lives, but also founded a flourishing publishing house. Today, staying true to this spirit, Collins books are packed with inspiration, innovation and practical expertise. They place you at the centre of a world of possibility and give you exactly what you need to explore it.

10 9 8 7 6 5 4 3

ISBN 978-0-00-839713-5

Collins® and COBUILD® are registered trademarks of HarperCollins*Publishers* Limited

www.collins.co.uk/elt

British Library Cataloguing in Publication Data

A catalogue record for this publication is available from the British Library.

Author: Katie Foufouti
Illustrator: Roy Hermelin (Beehive)
Series editor: Rebecca Adlard
Commissioning editor: Zoë Clarke
Publishing manager: Lisa Todd
Product managers: Jennifer Hall and Caroline Green
In-house editor: Alma Puts Keren
Project manager: Emily Hooton
Editor: Barbara MacKay
Proofreaders: Natalie Murray and Michael Lamb
Cover designer: Kevin Robbins
Typesetter: 2Hoots Publishing Services Ltd
Audio produced by id audio, London
Reading guide author: Emma Wilkinson
Production controller: Rachel Weaver
Printed and bound in the UK by Pureprint

MIX
Paper | Supporting responsible forestry
FSC
www.fsc.org
FSC™ C007454

This book contains FSC™ certified paper and other controlled sources to ensure responsible forest management.

For more information visit: www.harpercollins.co.uk/green

Download the audio for this book and a reading guide for parents and teachers at www.collins.co.uk/839713